Ups
and
Downs
A Book of Emotions

Mike Wohnoutka

CANDLEWICK PRESS

Sleepy

AWAKE

Delighted

Disgusted

Excited

Scared

Relaxed

RING!‒

Stressed

Pleased

Jealous

Lonely

Can I sit here?

Hopeful

Connected

Embarrassed

Thank you.

Comforted

Worried

Confident

ENERGETIC

Peaceful

Surprised

CRASH

Regretful

Apologetic

I'm sorry.

Annoyed

Flattered

Disappointed

Cheerful

Bored

Curious

Awkward

Shy

Friendly

Joyful!

To Franklin and Olivia—wishing you more ups than downs

First edition 2023

Library of Congress Catalog Card Number 2022923389
ISBN 978-1-5362-2737-6

23 24 25 26 27 28 APS 10 9 8 7 6 5 4 3 2 1

Printed in Humen, Dongguan, China

This book was typeset in Radley.
The illustrations were done in gouache.

Candlewick Press
99 Dover Street
Somerville, Massachusetts 02144

www.candlewick.com